leapfrog

Rhyme
Time

Big Bad Bart

First published in 2006 by
Franklin Watts
338 Euston Road
London
NW1 3BH

Franklin Watts Australia
Hachette Children's Books
Level 17/207 Kent Street
Sydney
NSW 2000

A CIP catalogue record for this book is available
from the British Library.

ISBN (10) 0 7496 6599 8 (hbk)
ISBN (13) 978-0-7496-6599-9 (hbk)
ISBN (10) 0 7496 6816 4 (pbk)
ISBN (13) 978-0-7496-6816-7 (pbk)

Series Editor: Jackie Hamley
Series Advisor: Dr Barrie Wade
Series Designer: Peter Scoulding

Printed in China

Leapfrog
Rhyme
Time

Big Bad Bart

by Damian Harvey

Illustrated by Fabiano Fiorin

W
FRANKLIN WATTS
LONDON•SYDNEY

When Big Bad Bart

rides into town

with a scarf round his face

and his hat pulled down ...

... people scream
and people shout:

"You'd better watch out,
Bad Bart's about!"

Windows close and doors soon slam.

Even the cats and dogs
all scram.

9

In the prison cells
they shake with fear.

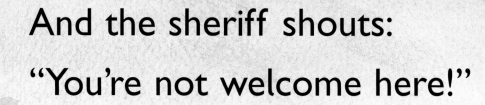

And the sheriff shouts:

"You're not welcome here!"

But Big Bad Bart's
heard it all before,

14

and he walks right
through the saloon door.

From over one shoulder

Bart pulls a guitar,

16

and starts to play
like a real rock star.

People dance as
the music plays.

19

But Big Bad Bart gets
carried away.

At the top of his voice,
he starts to sing.

He howls and he wails,
just like a wild thing.

Windows break and glasses shatter.

He even makes Hank's
false teeth chatter!

Then people scream
and people shout:

"That's enough Bad Bart!
Now get on out!"

So Big Bad Bart
gets sent away,

to where only wolves
can hear him play.

But late at night, by the
light of the moon,

you might just hear
him howl a tune!

Leapfrog has been specially designed to fit the requirements of the National Literacy Strategy. It offers real books for beginning readers by top authors and illustrators.

There are 55 Leapfrog stories to choose from:

The Bossy Cockerel
ISBN 0 7496 3828 1

Bill's Baggy Trousers
ISBN 0 7496 3829 X

Mr Spotty's Potty
ISBN 0 7496 3831 1

Little Joe's Big Race
ISBN 0 7496 3832 X

The Little Star
ISBN 0 7496 3833 8

The Cheeky Monkey
ISBN 0 7496 3830 3

Selfish Sophie
ISBN 0 7496 4385 4

Recycled!
ISBN 0 7496 4388 9

Felix on the Move
ISBN 0 7496 4387 0

Pippa and Poppa
ISBN 0 7496 4386 2

Jack's Party
ISBN 0 7496 4389 7

The Best Snowman
ISBN 0 7496 4390 0

Eight Enormous Elephants
ISBN 0 7496 4634 9

Mary and the Fairy
ISBN 0 7496 4633 0

The Crying Princess
ISBN 0 7496 4632 2

Jasper and Jess
ISBN 0 7496 4081 2

The Lazy Scarecrow
ISBN 0 7496 4082 0

The Naughty Puppy
ISBN 0 7496 4383 8

Freddie's Fears
ISBN 0 7496 4382 X

FAIRY TALES

Cinderella
ISBN 0 7496 4228 9

The Three Little Pigs
ISBN 0 7496 4227 0

Jack and the Beanstalk
ISBN 0 7496 4229 7

The Three Billy Goats Gruff
ISBN 0 7496 4226 2

Goldilocks and the Three Bears
ISBN 0 7496 4225 4

Little Red Riding Hood
ISBN 0 7496 4224 6

Rapunzel
ISBN 0 7496 6159 3

Snow White
ISBN 0 7496 6161 5

The Emperor's New Clothes
ISBN 0 7496 6163 1

The Pied Piper of Hamelin
ISBN 0 7496 6164 X

Hansel and Gretel
ISBN 0 7496 6162 3

The Sleeping Beauty
ISBN 0 7496 6160 7

Rumpelstiltskin
ISBN 0 7496 6165 8

The Ugly Duckling
ISBN 0 7496 6166 6

Puss in Boots
ISBN 0 7496 6167 4

The Frog Prince
ISBN 0 7496 6168 2

The Princess and the Pea
ISBN 0 7496 6169 0

Dick Whittington
ISBN 0 7496 6170 4

The Elves and the Shoemaker
ISBN 0 7496 6575 0*
ISBN 0 7496 6581 5

The Little Match Girl
ISBN 0 7496 6576 9*
ISBN 0 7496 6582 3

The Little Mermaid
ISBN 0 7496 6577 7*
ISBN 0 7496 6583 1

The Little Red Hen
ISBN 0 7496 6578 5*
ISBN 0 7496 6585 8

The Nightingale
ISBN 0 7496 6579 3*
ISBN 0 7496 6586 6

Thumbelina
ISBN 0 7496 6580 7*
ISBN 0 7496 6587 4

RHYME TIME

Squeaky Clean
ISBN 0 7496 6805 9

Craig's Crocodile
ISBN 0 7496 6806 7

Felicity Floss: Tooth Fairy
ISBN 0 7496 6807 5

Captain Cool
ISBN 0 7496 6808 3

Monster Cake
ISBN 0 7496 6809 1

The Super Trolley Ride
ISBN 0 7496 6810 5

The Royal Jumble Sale
ISBN 0 7496 6594 7*
ISBN 0 7496 6811 3

But, Mum!
ISBN 0 7496 6595 5*
ISBN 0 7496 6812 1

Dan's Gran's Goat
ISBN 0 7496 6596 3*
ISBN 0 7496 6814 8

Lighthouse Mouse
ISBN 0 7496 6597 1*
ISBN 0 7496 6815 6

Big Bad Bart
ISBN 0 7496 6599 8*
ISBN 0 7496 6816 4

Ron's Race
ISBN 0 7496 6600 5*
ISBN 0 7496 6817 2

* hardback